TBA2183

D0347180

This Little Tiger book belongs to:

_____

_____

_____

For Roan, with love
— R G

LITTLE TIGER PRESS

An imprint of Magi Publications

1 The Coda Centre, 189 Munster Road, London SW6 6AW

www.littletigerpress.com

First published in Great Britain 2007
This edition published 2007

Text and illustrations copyright © Ruth Galloway 2007
Ruth Galloway has asserted her rights to be identified as the author
and illustrator of this work under the Copyright,
Designs and Patents Act, 1988

A CIP catalogue record for this book is available from the British Library

All rights reserved • ISBN 978-1-84506-376-4

Printed in Belgium

2 4 6 8 10 9 7 5 3

Tickly Octopus

Ruth Galloway

LITTLE TIGER PRESS
London

Down in the ocean, among the swirling
seaweed and the colourful coral,
lived a tickly octopus.

He had eight twisty, twirly tentacles
and he loved to use them to tickle.

When Octopus tickled the little fish
they jumped and jiggled and wriggled and giggled!
They thought tickling was wonderful fun!

But most of the creatures
found his tickling tiresome.

Octopus tickled Starfish
and made her squirm!
"Stop it," she squeaked.

Octopus tickled the
clickety-clackety crab and
he tripped and tumbled
into the sand.
"Go away!" he snapped.

"But I'm a tickly octopus, and I'm really good at tickling," said Octopus sadly, and he swam off to tickle the wriggly, giggly fish again.

One day Octopus saw Oyster snoozing among the seashells. He couldn't resist giving her just a teeny tiny tickle.

But Oyster woke with
a jump and dropped her precious pearl.
PING! BIP! BOING! It bounced over
the rocks and was swept away by the current.
"Oh no!" gasped Octopus.
Poor Oyster was very upset.
"Sorry!" said Octopus. "I'll get it back for you."

Octopus raced through the water
with a WHOOSH! and a SWOOSH!
"Whee!" he thought. "I never knew I could
be so super speedy!"

Octopus followed the pearl as it tumbled
down to the bottom of the sea.
"Wow!" he thought. "I never knew
I could swim so deep!"

At last Octopus reached
the pearl but . . .

PLINK!
PLONK!
PLOP!

Oyster's precious pearl bounced
over the rocks and dropped
down through a tiny gap in
the ocean floor.

Octopus squished and squashed
and heaved and squeezed . . .

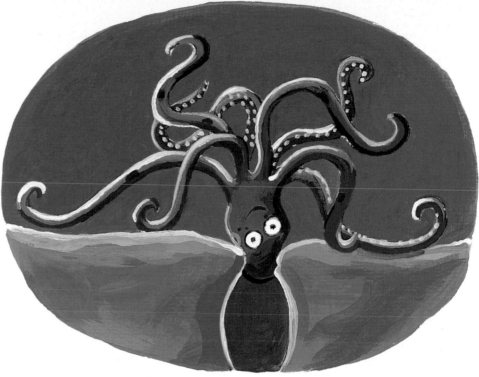

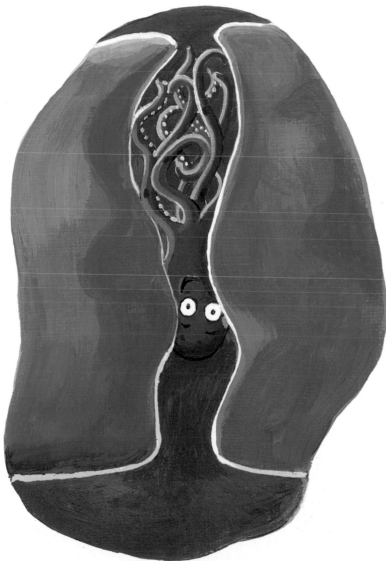

and managed to push his
rubbery body through the gap.

"Ooh!" he thought. "I never knew
I could be so squidgy!"

There, glinting in the darkness, was
the smooth and shiny pearl. But just
behind it was a fierce eel.

"Aaargh!" squeaked Octopus.
He quickly picked up the pearl
and sped away.

"GIVE ME THAT PEARL!"
roared the eel.

Octopus huffed and puffed as the eel chased after him.
He'd swum such a long way and he was very tired.
The eel was getting closer and closer...

With a spurt and a squirt, a belch and
a squelch, Octopus sprayed a cloud of black
ink so that the eel couldn't see a thing!

"Wow!" thought Octopus.
"I never knew I could be so inky."
And he danced happily back to Oyster.

Oyster was delighted to get her pearl back.

"I promise I won't ever tickle you again," Octopus said.

"I've found lots of other things I'm good at doing too.

From now on I'm going to be a . . ."

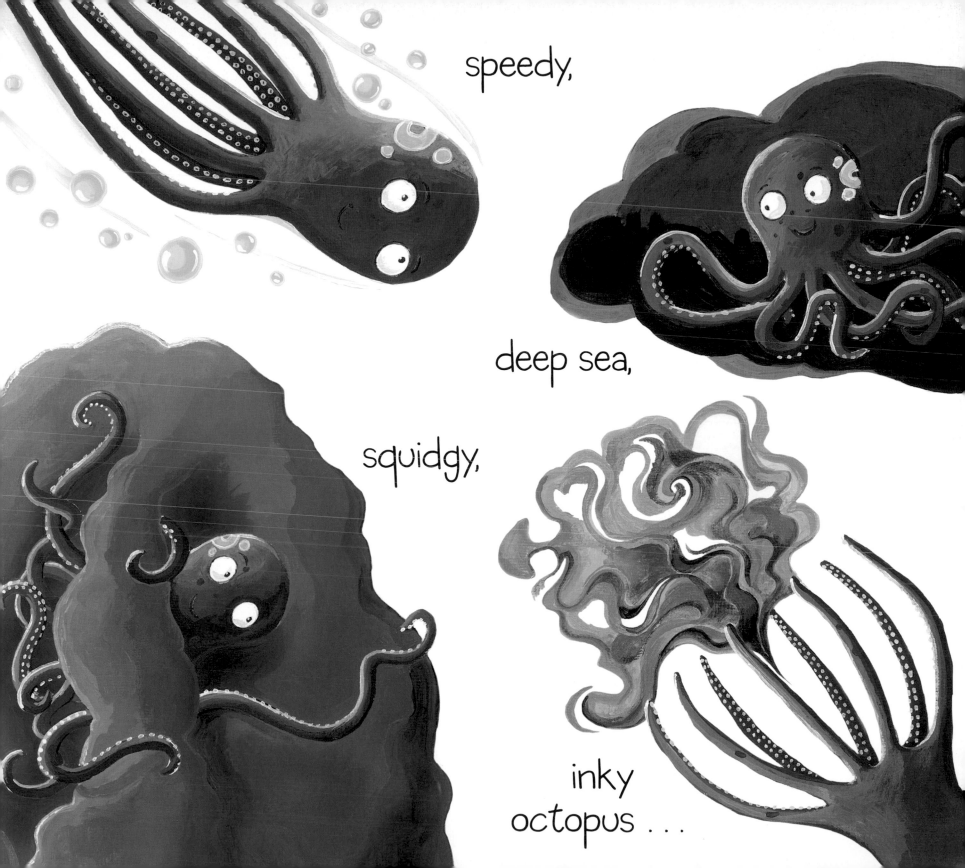

speedy,

deep sea,

squidgy,

inky
octopus . . .

"... but I'll still be a little bit tickly, too!"

Books to make you *giggle* from Little Tiger Press

The Very Greedy Bee
Steve Smallman   Jack Tickle

I'm Not Going Out There!
PAUL BRIGHT   BEN CORT

Clumsy Crab
Ruth Galloway

cock-a-doodle-hooooooo!
Mick Manning   Brita Granström

Smiley Shark
Ruth Galloway

Me and My Dad!
Alison Ritchie
illustrated by
Alison Edgson

For information regarding any of the above titles
or for our catalogue, please contact us:
Little Tiger Press, 1 The Coda Centre,
189 Munster Road, London SW6 6AW
Tel: 020 7385 6333 Fax: 020 7385 7333
E-mail: info@littletiger.co.uk
www.littletigerpress.com